Lizzie McGuire MYSTERIES

Spring It On!

By Samantha Maridan

Based on the television series, "Lizzie McGuire", created by Terri Minsky

Watch it on

Disney CHANNEL   abc Kids

Disney PRESS

VOLO

New York

Printed in the United States of America

First Edition
1 3 5 7 9 10 8 6 4 2

Library of Congress Catalog Card Number: 2004114349

ISBN 0-7868-4701-8
For more Disney Press fun, visit www.disneybooks.com
Visit DisneyChannel.com

"Did you ever notice how the auditorium is the most depressing room in the school?" asked Miranda Sanchez, Lizzie McGuire's best friend. Miranda was sitting between Lizzie and Lizzie's other best friend, David "Gordo" Gordon. They were waiting for the Friday morning assembly to begin.

"The walls are bore-me beige," Miranda went on. "The stage curtains match the walls, except they're dirtier. And there are no windows."

"I'm glad there are no windows," Lizzie said.

"Because if there were, you know what we'd see? Rain and more rain." It had been raining for the last two weeks, and Lizzie was seriously sick of it.

"The auditorium isn't any more boring than any other room in the school," Gordo said. "It just doesn't have any pizzazz—no decorative molding, arched doorways, recessed lighting—"

Where, Lizzie wondered, did he get all these terms? Then again, Gordo knew all sorts of bizarre things.

"What he means," Miranda translated, "is that there's nothing interesting about this room except—" A wicked look came into Miranda's dark eyes. "Him."

"Him?" Lizzie and Gordo asked together.

Miranda put her fingers to her lips and tilted her head toward Hal Walters, the new boy in their class, who was sitting three rows away from them. "I think he's hot," Miranda said in a low voice.

"Totally," Lizzie agreed, "in that bad-boy kind of way."

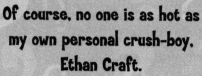 

Of course, no one is as hot as my own personal crush-boy, Ethan Craft.

"Hal's definitely got the coolness factor," Miranda said in a dreamy voice. "He looks like he should play lead guitar in a band."

"Exactly what about him looks musical to you?" Gordo asked.

Miranda didn't answer at first, but Lizzie knew what she meant. Hal Walters had jade green eyes and straight black hair. He was too skinny to be buff, but he was also kind of muscular, with really nice arms. Lizzie knew this because Hal always wore jeans and black T-shirts. And a leather wristband. Miranda was right—he definitely looked like the lead-guitar type.

"Maybe musical isn't the right word. It's hard

to find the right word for Hal," Miranda said. "Maybe soulful or stellar-cool . . ."

"I never should have asked," Gordo muttered.

"So have you two actually talked?" Lizzie asked.

Miranda sighed. "Not exactly. Hal is still an unrequited crush-from-afar."

"Not you, too," Gordo said. "It's bad enough that Lizzie is still pining over Ethan. Miranda, please, just ask Hal out."

Before Miranda could respond, Mr. Tweedy, the school principal, stepped to the front of the stage and began tapping on the microphone. "Testing," he said, "testing, one, two, three . . ."

Gordo sighed. "Just once I'd love to see him skip the 'testing' routine."

Mr. Tweedy frowned at the sheaf of papers in his hand. "My first announcement is that today's pep rally is canceled due to all the rain."

A few boys booed, but the principal silenced them with a look. "I'm afraid this can't be helped," he explained. "The game is also postponed until the rain lets up and the ground dries out. It's just too wet. I'll let you know as soon as it's rescheduled. And Kate Sanders, our head cheerleader, will let everyone know when the pep rally is rescheduled."

Kate Sanders—tall, blond, beautiful, and the Queen of Mean—stood up, and most of the kids applauded. Lizzie considered sticking her finger down her throat and making gagging motions. She decided not to. It was just too immature.

Just call me the
Queen of Mature.

"Also," Mr. Tweedy went on, "Coach Kelley will be at a conference for the next week, so all gym classes are canceled. You'll have study hall instead."

Yes! An entire week without the gym-nauseum.

"Final announcement," the principal said. "I've chosen a theme for our Spring Fling dance."

Suddenly, Miranda's hand clamped down on Lizzie's wrist in a death grip. "Oh, let it be mine, please let it be mine. Please pick my idea," she murmured.

"The competition was stiff this year," Principal Tweedy continued. "We had twelve entries. And I had a very hard time deciding. But the winner is—" He pushed his glasses up on his nose and flipped through his papers.

Miranda's hold on Lizzie's wrist tightened. "Flower Power," she said quietly, as if she were trying to hypnotize the principal. "Flower Power . . ."

"Miranda," Lizzie whispered, "you're cutting off my circulation."

"Sorry." Miranda let go of Lizzie's wrist.

"Ah, here it is!" The principal pulled a paper from his sheaf and smiled. "The winner is Miranda Sanchez, whose theme for the dance is Flower Power."

"Omigosh!" Miranda exclaimed as her eyes went wide with disbelief.

"You won!" Lizzie shrieked, and hugged her friend.

"Miranda's essay is what convinced me," Principal Tweedy explained. "I'd like to share a bit of it with you. 'Flowers are nature's bling-bling,'" he read aloud. "'They give everything color and fragrance and total, awesome beauty. My idea is to bring the feeling of a twilight spring evening into the gym. Imagine green paths, garlands of flowers, and the scent of lilacs in the air. . . .'"

Lizzie glanced at her friend. Miranda was glowing with pride.

"So, Miranda, the school will give you a

seventy-five-dollar budget to work with. We wish you luck!" Principal Tweedy said. "Everyone else, we'll see you at the dance one week from Saturday! Today's assembly is dismissed."

Most of the students headed off toward their first-period classes, but Miranda stayed in her seat. She looked too dazed to get up. "That's eight days," Miranda said slowly. "We've got exactly eight days to work Flower Power magic!"

"Um, I hate to be the one to break it to you," Gordo said, "but somebody—actually quite a few somebodies—are not happy about this. I bet Kate had one of the eleven ideas that weren't chosen."

Kate and her evil crew were all aiming death-ray glares at Miranda.

"Forget them. We've got to move fast," Miranda said. "There's a ton of stuff to do before next Saturday."

"We?" Lizzie echoed.

"You and Gordo are my Spring Fling committee—the Flower Power posse. Aren't you?"

"Uh—" Lizzie stammered. It wasn't that she didn't want to help Miranda. She just had sort of an allergic reaction to the gym-nauseum.

I'm really expected to spend a week fixing up a room where I have experienced maximum humiliation?

"Lizzie, you're already stylin' for it," Miranda pointed out. "Look at what you're wearing."

Lizzie looked. She was wearing a white, long-sleeved T-shirt with a big sparkly pink flower across her chest, and low-rise jeans with pink and green flowers embroidered down the side seams. Even worse, her headband had tiny pink rhinestone flowers all across it.

Did I have to wear this today? Couldn't I have worn my DEATH TO MATH! T-shirt?

"And, Gordo, you already know all that stuff about interior design, which is going to be perfecto for decorating the gym," Miranda went on.

Gordo shot Lizzie a panicked look.

"Besides," Miranda said, "it's going to be so great. We're going to have trees and garden paths lit by glowing lanterns—"

"Miranda, this is the school gym you're talking about," Lizzie reminded her.

"No problema," said Miranda. "I've got it all planned."

"Oh, you're going to have problems, all right." It was Kate Sanders. The she-beast had sneaked up behind them. "Flower Power is a totally lame idea," she declared. "You just watch. Flower Power will wilt before the night of the dance. It's going to be so over before it even starts."

Lizzie opened her lunch bag and took out her sandwich. She didn't have to unwrap it to know that something was wrong. It was round. It had to be her little brother Matt's creation. She unwrapped the foil and stared at a liverwurst-and-peanut-butter sandwich with pickles.

Does he try to be disgusting? Or does it just come naturally?

Lizzie felt sick to her stomach. "He does this deliberately," she muttered. "My pointy-headed little brother knows I hate his revolting sandwiches and—"

"Are you talking to yourself?" Miranda slid into the seat beside her.

"Somehow," Lizzie said, "I got rat-breath's lunch."

Miranda wrinkled her nose. "Want to share mine? I've got a topopo salad—there's plenty." Miranda opened a container that was filled with lettuce, tomatoes, tortilla chips, shredded cheese, and strips of broiled chicken.

"You're a true bud," Lizzie said. "Let me just grab a fork."

Lizzie and Miranda dug into the salad and ate in silence. Finally, Miranda said, "Are you okay? You've looked kind of blue all morning."

Lizzie considered this. "You know what the real problem is?" she asked. "It's the rain. My hair has been frizzing for two weeks straight. My books are soggy. My sneakers smell like mildew. And everyone looks drippy to me."

"Even Ethan?" Miranda asked.

Ethan Craft was sitting at a table on the other side of the cafeteria. With sun-streaked hair and tanned skin, Ethan looked anything but drippy.

Lizzie smiled dreamily. "Everyone *except* Ethan."

"Are you going to ask Ethan to Spring Fling?" Miranda asked.

"Not in this lifetime," Lizzie replied. "Don't you remember what happened last time?"

Long story short: Ethan turned me down. Twice! Does it get any more humiliating?

"Yeah, but he could have a change of heart," Miranda said. "Picture this. The gym is totally transformed into this moonlit garden. You and Ethan are surrounded by all these beautiful flowers, and it's the most romantic place ever. So romantic that he draws you close and bends his head to kiss—"

"Okay, okay, I get the picture," Lizzie said quickly. She could feel herself blushing. "It's not as if I don't want to go with him—"

Gordo set his lunch tray on the table and sat down beside Lizzie. "Can I quote you on that?"

"No, you cannot," Lizzie said firmly.

"You don't understand. This is for an extra-credit project for my sociology class," Gordo explained. "I'm doing a study of student dating methods."

"Obviously, I don't qualify for your study," Lizzie told him. "I have no dating methods."

And the proof is: I have no dates. This is the most depressing thing on Earth to be able to prove.

"How about you, Miranda?" Gordo asked. "What are your dating strategies?"

Miranda sipped the last of her milk. "Mine haven't worked so well, either," she admitted. "New plan needed." She nodded toward Hal Walters, who was sitting with Larry Tudgeman and Jolie Johnson. They were both major computer geeks, but Jolie, a seventh grader, was kind of cute for a geek. And Jolie was looking at Hal as if he were the most gorgeous guy ever.

"I'm not going to wait for Hal to ask me," Miranda declared. "And I'm not going to put him on the spot and ask him out, either."

"This could be interesting." Gordo pulled his camcorder from his pack and turned it on. "Miranda Sanchez has decided to avoid the whole asking-out drama. So, Miranda, what are you going to do?"

Miranda rolled her eyes at the camcorder. "It's simple. I'm going to get involved in something Hal does or—even better—invite him to do something I'm interested in, so we can hang out together with no pressure."

"See?" Gordo said to Lizzie. "All you have to do is get involved in something Ethan does, something the two of you can do together."

"Like what?" Lizzie asked.

Her friends stared at her blankly.

Gordo turned back to Miranda. "I know what you can ask Hal to do—invite him to join the Flower Power posse."

Miranda shook her head. "I don't think so. I mean, what guy is going to want to decorate a gym—" She caught herself. "Present company excepted."

"You know," Lizzie said thoughtfully, "it's probably worth asking. I mean, Hal just started school here, and it looks like the only people he knows are Jolie and the Tudge, who are okay if you like dweebs. Hal might be really relieved to have a chance to hang out with some normals."

"True," Gordo said encouragingly.

"Fine, I will." Miranda stood up with a flounce and walked straight over to Hal's table.

"Awesome," Gordo murmured as he watched Miranda talking with Hal. "No one can say our Miranda doesn't have guts."

Miranda returned to their table a few minutes later, a strange look on her face.

"Well?" Lizzie asked. "What did he say?"

"Hal said yes," Miranda reported. "He said working on the dance sounded totally cool. There's just one catch. Jolie said yes, too."

Lizzie stood at her locker, trying to decide which books to take home for the weekend.

"Good news, *chica*." Miranda came up to her. "I talked to Gordo, Hal, and Jolie, and the first meeting of the Flower Power posse will be at one tomorrow in the gym."

"On a Saturday?" Lizzie cried. "We have to come to school on the weekend?"

"We've got to start decking out the gym,"

Miranda told her. "I am so totally psyched!"

Lizzie was not equally psyched, but she could see how much Spring Fling meant to her friend. "Okay," she agreed, "I'll be there."

She put on her pink see-through rain slicker, stuffed her books in her bag, and turned to leave. Someone behind them shouted, "Lizzie, Miranda, wait up!"

Lizzie turned and saw Tudgeman running toward them. "You've got to come see what's on the school Web site!" he told them.

Lizzie and Miranda followed Tudgeman to the computer lab and stared at the screen. It read:

```
To: everyone who matters—you know
    who you are
From: wiseup
Subject: next saturday night

listen up. flower power is pathetic.
so prove you've got some class.
don't go to spring fling—we all
know it's going to flop!
```

Lizzie couldn't believe it. How dare someone dis Miranda's idea this way?

Hmm, maybe I'll have another case to solve.

Lizzie wasn't exactly a professional detective, but she had solved a few mysteries for her friends. And she couldn't help feeling a buzz of excitement now that another mystery seemed to be popping up.

"Who is 'wiseup'?" Lizzie mused aloud.

"And why does she have it in for Spring Fling?" Miranda added heatedly.

"Could be a he," Tudgeman pointed out.

"What makes you think so?" Lizzie asked. She wished she had her special detective notebook with her. She would have to write everything down when she got home.

"Not everyone can post a message to the Forum," Tudgeman explained.

"So who can?" Lizzie asked.

Tudgeman hesitated a moment. "Well, the Webmasters, who maintain the school's Web site—"

"Like you," Miranda said.

Tudgeman nodded. "Webmasters and students who are in charge of activities. They have access codes to post important notices."

"Like Kate," Miranda said. "She posts stuff about tryouts and pep rallies."

"Or it could have been hacked," the Tudge said.

Lizzie's brain was clicking into detective mode. "So, can you trace this message to whoever sent it?"

The Tudge was brilliant when it came to computers. He shook his head. "I tried, but whoever sent this knew what they were doing."

"That message has the Queen of Mean written all over it," Miranda said angrily. "Kate Sanders can't deal with the fact that Principal Tweedy chose my idea over hers."

"Highly possible. But we don't know that for sure," Lizzie reasoned. "I mean, Principal Tweedy said he got twelve ideas for the dance. That means there could be eleven sore losers in Hillridge. Plus, there's Kate's evil crew. Any one of them might have done this just to kiss up to her."

Tudgeman nodded solemnly. "Good points."

Miranda stared at the screen. "Why would anyone want to do this?" she asked sadly.

Suddenly, Lizzie, who had not been all that

enthusiastic about working on the dance, knew she had to be part of the Flower Power posse. She wasn't going to let anyone ruin Miranda's big night.

"We're not going to take this," Lizzie assured her friend. "Tudgeman, we need your help. Can you make that evil message disappear?"

"Affirmative!" Tudgeman replied and punched a few keys. The message vanished.

"Perfect," Lizzie said. "Now, we need you to post a reply. One that no one else can trace."

Moments later, Lizzie's message was on the site. It read:

```
wiseup, watch out! flower power
is going to rock! be there or
be borrr-rring!
```

On Saturday afternoon, Lizzie arrived at Hillridge Junior High. Her hair was frizzed, her shoes were soaked, and her pants were muddy.

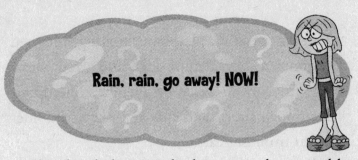

Rain, rain, go away! NOW!

She headed toward the gym, her muddy footprints joining a trail of others. The junior high, she realized, was a busy place on Saturdays. She could hear singing in the auditorium and saw a group of kids painting in the art room.

Hal was already in the gym. He was sitting on the bottom step of the bleachers, his face tilted up. He seemed to be studying the cinder-block walls. Jolie was there, too. She was studying Hal.

"Doesn't look anything like a garden in here," Hal observed. "It's going to be impressive if we can really pull this off."

"Miranda can," Lizzie said loyally. "She always has great ideas."

"I hope there are lots of red flowers," Jolie said. "Red is my favorite color."

Lizzie noticed that Jolie was wearing shiny red rain boots, a short denim skirt, and a red sweatshirt with a white kitten on it. Jolie's blond hair was cropped short, and tiny red plastic bunnies dangled from her ears.

Jolie tapped the keys of her handheld computer, then showed it to Lizzie.

Lizzie squinted at the tiny screen and saw a photo of a white puppy surrounded by red roses.

"I can print up dozens of those at home," Jolie told her. "And then we can pin them all over the walls. Don't you think spring is really all about puppies and bunnies and kittens?"

Uh, no. But I have a feeling that's the wrong answer.

At that moment, the gym doors opened, and Miranda and Gordo came in. Miranda was loaded down with shopping bags. Gordo was carrying a metal toolbox in one hand and a small stepladder in the other. He heaved the toolbox onto the bleachers, then sat down beside it.

"Welcome to the first meeting of the Flower Power posse!" Miranda began. "Today I want to start on some of the non-live flower decorations."

Jolie looked crestfallen. "No real flowers?"

"This whole thing is about real flowers," Miranda assured her. "But they only last a day or two, so we can't bring the real ones in until next Friday and Saturday. In the meantime, there's plenty we can do. I was thinking lighting." Miranda reached into one of the shopping bags and pulled out long strands of Japanese paper lanterns. She plugged one into an electrical outlet, and it glowed pink and blue and green. "We could put these up on the walls."

"How about this?" Hal picked up a string of lanterns. "We use four strands of lights—two going from the front of the gym to the middle of the side walls, and same thing from the back of the gym. It will be a diamond of colored lights."

"Sounds good," Miranda said. "Let's give it a try."

Gordo took a hammer and some nails from his toolbox, and they began to string up the lights. Hanging the lanterns up on the side walls was easy because they could stand on the bleachers. But for the front and back walls of the gym, Gordo's stepladder was too short.

"We need a real ladder," said Hal. "Anyone know where we can get one?"

Lizzie knew. But she wasn't about to say.

Gordo spoke the fateful words. "The only ladder in the school is in the janitor's supply closet. And, in case you don't know, Mr. Zaber, our janitor, is one of the crankiest people on the planet."

"Totally true," Lizzie agreed. "Mr. Zaber would not appreciate it if we borrowed his stuff."

"Except he'll never know," Hal pointed out. "I

mean, it's Saturday. We'll use the ladder now and then put it back exactly where we found it. He'll come in Monday morning and never notice."

Um, does anyone actually believe that?

Lizzie turned to Miranda. "You know how grouchy Mr. Zaber is."

"Lizzie's right," Miranda said. Her eyes locked on Hal. "We can only do this if you're a zillion percent sure he'll never notice."

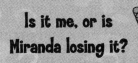

Is it me, or is Miranda losing it?

"No problem," Hal said. "Just tell me where the supply closet is."

Gordo gave Hal directions to the janitor's closet, and Hal disappeared. Five minutes later, he returned with the ladder.

They finished hanging the lanterns and began to make big flowers out of sheets of colored crepe paper. "We'll put these on the sides of the bleachers," Miranda explained. She demonstrated how to cut and fold the crepe paper and then wrap the base in wire so that it opened into a flower. To Lizzie's surprise, the flower-making was fun and easy. Soon, the gym floor was covered with a field of colorful flowers.

"This is fantabulous!" Jolie said as she made a bouquet of giant red blooms.

"It is pretty nifty," Hal admitted. He was layering the crepe paper so that each flower had shades of yellow and pink and orange. "It's weird, though. I never imagined myself making paper flowers."

"You've got a definite talent for it," Miranda told him with a smile.

"Yeah." Hal gave her a lopsided grin. "Who knew?"

Since Hal and Miranda were getting along, and Jolie seemed absorbed in using every piece of red crepe paper in the room, Lizzie figured it was a good time to talk to Gordo.

"How goes it?" Lizzie asked.

"Not good," Gordo replied. "Every time I try to wrap the wire around the crepe paper, I either tear a hole in the paper or stick myself in the thumb."

"Well, then, how's the sociology project coming?" Lizzie asked.

"Not bad. I'm uncovering some interesting techniques for getting dates."

"Such as?"

Gordo tried not to smile. "You're not going to want to try any of this stuff with Ethan, I guarantee it."

"What stuff?" Lizzie tried not to look too eager.

> **This could be it—the key to getting Ethan to realize he's majorly crushing on me.**

"Okay." Gordo stopped making flowers. "One girl invited the guy she liked to a karaoke fest."

"Me sing aloud with Ethan watching? Next idea."

"Tudgeman came up with a foolproof method. He challenged all his potential dates to a *Star Wars* trivia quiz. He said this girl Greta beat him twice, and he knew it was true love."

"Definitely not an option," Lizzie said.

Gordo tilted his head toward Miranda and Hal. "I think Miranda's strategy might be working."

Miranda and Hal were laughing as they pinned the paper flowers to the sides of the bleachers, though Lizzie noticed that every time they got a few flowers up, Hal rearranged them.

"Interesting." Gordo had noticed the same thing. "Hal's arranging the flowers by hue. It looks good."

"What are you kids doing with my ladder?" an angry voice behind them demanded. Lizzie turned and saw Mr. Zaber standing in the doorway, scowling down at the Flower Power posse.

Miranda turned to face him. "I'm the one responsible, Mr. Zaber. We're just getting the gym ready for next weekend's Spring Fling dance. Principal Tweedy knows we're here."

"Does he know you're using my ladder without my permission?" the janitor inquired.

"Well—" Miranda hedged.

"I don't have time for excuses. I'm about to leave and lock up the building, so, all of you, clean up this mess, then get out."

"B-but—" Miranda sputtered.

"Please, Mr. Zaber," Lizzie chimed in. "We've only got a week to get ready for the dance."

The janitor's eyebrows lowered until they looked like one thick brow. "I'm taking my ladder back. It's not safe for you kids to use it. If one of you got hurt, you know who'd be held responsible? Me!"

"We're really sorry about that," Miranda said. "But couldn't we just work here a little longer?"

"I'll give you half an hour. Not a minute more." Mr. Zaber grabbed his ladder and stormed out of the gym.

Hal gave a low whistle. "You two are good. Can I hire you to talk to my parents for me?"

Lizzie remembered the time she and Miranda had tried to talk their parents out of sending them to Camp Bunsen Burner. "Trust me," she said, "you don't want to do that."

Lizzie had just made it to homeroom on Monday morning when an announcement crackled over the PA system. "Miranda Sanchez, David Gordon, Jolie Johnson, Hal Walters, and Lizzie McGuire, please report to the principal's office immediately."

Everyone turned to stare at Lizzie.

"What did you do?" Tudgeman asked.

"Oooh, Lizzie's in trouble now," Claire Miller crooned.

In a haze of embarrassment and dread, Lizzie found her way to the principal's office where Miranda, Gordo, Hal, and Jolie stood. Except for Hal, they all looked as frightened as Lizzie felt. They were facing a serious-looking Principal Tweedy—and a red-faced Mr. Zaber.

Uh-oh, Lizzie thought.

"Miss McGuire," Principal Tweedy said. "How kind of you to join us."

Double uh-oh, Lizzie thought.

"Do you all know why you're here?" he asked the group.

They all shook their heads.

"What did you do to my nice, clean gym?" the janitor demanded.

Miranda swallowed hard. "We hung up some lanterns and put up some paper flowers."

"Is that all?" the principal demanded.

Lizzie gathered up her courage. "Yes."

"We're going to take a little field trip," said the principal.

Lizzie's dread built as they walked single file through the halls. The walk seemed to take forever.

I never realized it's at least 70 miles from the principal's office to the gym.

At last Mr. Zaber threw open the double doors. The gym's wood floor was covered with shiny puddles of water. All the paper lanterns and the tissue-paper flowers were soaking wet—and completely ruined!

At first Lizzie couldn't take it in. "The gym ceiling has a leak?" she asked. She took another look at the floor. There were puddles everywhere. "A lot of leaks?"

Gordo shook his head. "Doubtful. It looks like someone set off the sprinkler system."

"Very perceptive, Mr. Gordon," the principal said.

Lizzie still couldn't make sense of it. "You mean, there was some kind of fire in here?"

"That's an excellent question," Principal

Tweedy said. "Was there?" He looked at each of them in turn.

Miranda spoke up. "Not while we were here on Saturday, if that's what you're asking."

"You're very certain of that?" Principal Tweedy said.

"Positive. No fire, no smoke. And when we left the gym it was totally dry," Jolie added.

"Why would we want to ruin the decorations we worked so hard to put up?" Miranda asked. "I used twenty-three dollars from the budget just to buy all those lanterns, and now they're totally ruined!"

Hal was staring at the ceiling. "Besides, how would we set off a sprinkler system?"

"Never mind that," the janitor grumbled.

"Can we go back to class now?" Jolie asked. "It's super-damp in here, and my hair is totally frizzing!"

Principal Tweedy looked from the four kids to the soggy floor. "I think you should all help clean this up. Then you can go back to class. Mr. Zaber has kindly provided some extra mops. And there will be no after-school meeting in the gym today. We're going to have to check out the sprinkler system."

Lizzie took a mop. She had a feeling it was going to be a very long week.

I'm actually mopping my least-favorite room in the school. I get karma points for this, don't I?

At lunchtime, Lizzie found Miranda in the cafeteria, working on some sort of list.

"What's that?" Lizzie asked, sliding in beside her. She opened her own lunch—a container of honey yogurt, a fruit salad, and a brownie. She had packed it herself; totally Matt-proof.

"I've got to come up with new ideas for decorating the gym," Miranda said. "I spent twenty-three dollars on the lanterns, and another six on all the crepe paper and wire. That's more than a third of my budget gone! The water-sprinkler disaster may have ruined everything!"

"Hey, are those sounds of despair?" Hal walked up behind Miranda, touched her lightly on the shoulder, and took the chair on the other side of her. "What's up?"

Miranda explained, looking even more upset as she repeated the depressing numbers.

Lizzie really wanted to talk about the sprinkler incident, but she could see this wasn't the time. "Don't worry," she told her friend. "I'm sure we'll come up with some other cool ideas."

Miranda looked at her bleakly. "For instance—"

"Um—" Lizzie started thinking, but creating gardens in gyms wasn't really her area of expertise.

"How about little white Christmas lights?" Hal suggested. "My mom once used them for an outdoor party and everyone told her how pretty and romantic they looked."

The word romantic—and the sight of Ethan Craft walking into the cafeteria—was all it took for Lizzie's imagination to kick into high gear. She pictured the two of them in a moonlit garden. She was wearing a long filmy dress, and a circlet of delicate flowers was wound through her hair. They were moving toward each other in slow motion, their arms outstretched. It was completely romantic—and totally impossible!

She snapped out of it as Jolie joined them at the lunch table. "I bet my mom has some of those white lights in our attic," Jolie said. She pulled out her handheld computer and began tapping keys, muttering, "Note to self: bring lights to school tomorrow." She glanced up at Miranda. "What about our meeting today?"

Gordo pulled up a chair. "I vote we take a break and regroup tomorrow."

"A day off isn't a bad idea," Miranda said. "I

could visit some garden stores and see what kind of inexpensive flowers I can find. But since you're all here, let's go over some stuff now."

She opened a folder and took out a bunch of papers that she handed around. "This is what we have to do before Saturday. Take a look and let me know if there's anything you think we should change."

Lizzie looked at the long list in dismay. "When are we going to have time to string leis for the entire junior high?"

"Okay, maybe that's a little ambitious," Miranda agreed.

Gordo's hand went up. "I have a problem with number five—cut lilacs and arrange around gym. It's only April. Lilacs don't even start blooming for another month."

"Oh," Miranda said. "Scratch number five."

"What's number eleven—ponds?" Jolie asked.

"Look at this," Miranda said. She showed them a magazine photo of a ritzy party on a country estate. The women wore long gowns, the men tuxedos. But what Miranda was pointing at was a pond with candles and flowers floating on it.

Gordo raised one eyebrow. "You're suggesting we put a pond in the middle of the gym? Mr. Zaber's really going to love that one."

"Not a pond," Miranda said. "But something that looks countryish and rustic. Like old water troughs."

"And we'd find these where?" Lizzie wondered. "There aren't exactly any farms or ranches around here."

Hal studied the photo. "Maybe not, but I bet everyone has a metal bucket at home, and they're pretty rustic looking. We could each bring those in—"

"—and float little tea-light candles in them," Miranda finished, smiling at Hal.

"They're never going to let us use candles or anything with a flame," Gordo pointed out. "You know—school safety issues."

"Well, then we could just float flowers in them," said Miranda. "It would be like having flowers on a stream."

"Oh, exactly!" Jolie gushed. "It will be so," she smiled at Hal, "romantic! Do you have a computer?"

"Yeah, why?" Hal answered.

Jolie batted her eyelashes at him. "I just thought you should know that I'm really good at upgrading systems."

"Oh, man," Gordo muttered, "where's my camcorder when I need it?"

Lizzie saw her chance. "Why don't I walk you to your locker so you can get it?" she suggested.

"Sure," Gordo said.

The moment they were out of the cafeteria, Lizzie got to the point. "I've been thinking about the sprinklers," she told Gordo, "wondering what sets them off. Do you know?"

Gordo shrugged. "Could be someone on a ladder with a cigarette lighter. Or even someone who lit a fire in a trash can. I don't think it's that hard to set off a sprinkler system."

"That's what I was afraid of," Lizzie said with a sigh. "I can't believe it's a coincidence that as soon as we started to decorate the gym, something destroyed all our work. Wait a minute, what about Mr. Zaber?"

"What about him?" Gordo asked.

"He had to wait for us to leave, so he could lock up the school. So *we* weren't the last ones in the school. He was," said Lizzie. "But he tried to blame us, anyway. I think they call that deflecting suspicion."

Gordo's eyes widened. "Mr. Zaber is one of your suspects?"

"Not only one of them," Lizzie explained, "he just moved to the top of my list."

Lizzie's Tuesday did not start well. The first person she saw when she got to school was the Evil One. Kate was wearing a lavender sweater with a short, pale green skirt and diamond stud earrings. She looked perfect, as usual.

Can't Kate occasionally get a zit? Or frizzy hair? Is that really too much to ask?

The cheer-beast took one look at Lizzie and her eyes lit with malice. "Finally," Kate said, "you've learned to accessorize appropriately."

Lizzie didn't know what that meant, but whatever it was couldn't be good. She couldn't believe that back in grammar school, she and Kate had actually been buds.

"Your scrub bucket," Kate said, pointing to the metal pail Lizzie was holding. "Going to wash the floors? I hear you're awesome with a mop."

Lizzie's ears and face burned with embarrassment, but she didn't respond.

How come I can never think of a snappy comeback when I really need one?

Just then, Ethan walked by. He gave Lizzie a puzzled look and said, "Weird. I never knew you were so into cleaning, dude."

Lizzie wanted to scream. That was the most in-depth conversation she'd had with Ethan in weeks!

Maybe it was the Ice Queen's snarky remark, but Lizzie promptly demoted Mr. Zaber to Suspect Number Two and spent the whole morning wondering if Kate had been behind the sprinkler system disaster, especially since she also had access to the Web site. Not to mention a motive.

But in mystery novels, the bad guy is always the one you *don't* suspect. Maybe I should reconsider Mr. Zaber. . . . Maybe I need more information.

During afternoon study hall, Lizzie got a pass to the student activities room. Mr. Yamada, the faculty adviser, was standing in front of a white-board calendar, marking down student activities. The Spring Fling dance was already on it, along with a chess club match and a gymnastics meet.

"Lizzie," he said, "what can I do for you?"

"I was wondering if you could give me a list of the people who have access to the school Web site."

"Why would you need that?"

Lizzie improvised madly. "Well, for Spring Fling, we're making—corsages—for all the leaders of the student activities. To, kind of—thank them."

Mr. Yamada looked at her oddly, and for a moment Lizzie was sure he had seen through her lie. "Very well," he said. He sat down at the computer, typed in a few commands, and a list of students appeared.

Lizzie scanned the list. She zipped past the names of the kids who headed the Astronomy Club, the Future Nurses of America, and the band.

As head cheerleader, Kate Sanders had access to the Web site. No surprise there. Tudgeman's name was there as Webmaster—and so was Jolie Johnson's. She was a Web assistant!

Interesting, Lizzie thought. But she still had another lead to follow. "Mr. Yamada, can teachers or the school nurse or anyone else post to the site?"

Mr. Yamada scratched his head. "Actually, everyone on the faculty—from Principal Tweedy to Mr. Zaber—has access to it."

"Oh," Lizzie said. "I guess we'll need lots of corsages. Um—the corsages are kind of a secret, so please don't tell anyone, okay?"

"Your secret's safe with me," Mr. Yamada assured her.

Lizzie hoped he meant it. The last thing she needed was to actually have to come up with corsages for the dance.

In the meantime, she had to consider this new information. Somehow she couldn't picture

Tudgeman as a saboteur. But Kate was definitely on the list, and so was Mr. Zaber. And, she realized, so was Jolie.

When Lizzie got to the gym that afternoon, Hal stood on Mr. Zaber's ladder stringing white Christmas lights across the gym.

Jolie stood at the bottom of the ladder, handing the strands up to him. "This is such a brilliant idea," she cooed.

Miranda came up to Lizzie. "Who knew a computer geek could be such a flirt?" she whispered. She paused. "I guess I'm just a teensy bit jealous."

"I don't blame you," Lizzie said. "And Hal doesn't have to look like he's enjoying it so much. How did he get Mr. Zaber's ladder again, anyway?"

Gordo was sitting on the floor, trying to pry open a big cardboard box. "Hal said he borrowed it."

"And you believed that?" Lizzie asked.

Miranda glanced at Lizzie with a guilty expression. "Let's just say I didn't ask too many questions. I'm hoping we can just get the lights up quickly and return it."

Gordo gave a hard tug and the box came open. Inside were two large curved pieces of metal lattice and a small packet of nuts and bolts and washers.

"It's the arch I rented for the entrance to the gym!" Miranda said happily. "We're going to cover it with flowers, so it feels like you're walking into a garden."

"Now all we have to do is put it together." Gordo was looking through the box again. "It would be really nice if there were directions."

"The garden store said there would be directions," Miranda remarked. "I'm going to call and ask where they are."

She grabbed some quarters and trudged down the hall to use the pay phone by the office.

"I say we give it a whirl," Gordo told Lizzie.

He pulled a screwdriver out of his toolbox.

For about ten minutes Lizzie and Gordo tried to put the arch together. But there were four pieces that didn't seem to fit anywhere. And the arch wouldn't stand up. "We're doing something wrong," Gordo said.

"You think?" Lizzie asked. But she knew that she wasn't being much help. She kept getting distracted by Jolie, who was flirting up a storm with Hal.

"Gordo." Lizzie dropped her voice to a whisper. "I've got a theory."

"On how to put this together?" Gordo asked, looking delighted.

"No. On Jolie. She's totally competing with Miranda for Hal's attention. And she's an assistant Webmaster. She has access to the school Web site. So maybe she's the one who posted that creepy message."

"I don't know," Gordo said. "There are a lot of people who have access to that site. You're going to need better data. And speaking of data—" He let the word hang and gave Lizzie a meaningful look.

Lizzie had no idea what he was getting at. "What data?"

"I've been getting some interesting results with my dating survey," he explained. "You wouldn't believe how many girls ask boys out. And the boys like it. I mean, look at Miranda and Hal." Gordo's face flushed. "Or Jolie and Hal?"

"Shhh!" Lizzie said as Miranda came back into the gym.

"They're going to look for the directions," Miranda reported. "But they didn't sound very confident about finding them."

Hal came over to them and examined the arch. "Let's try something," he said. He picked up the four leftover pieces and examined them. "They're feet!" he exclaimed. "They hold the arch upright if we just connect it—" Within minutes Hal had figured out exactly how the arch needed to be put together.

"Amazing," Gordo said.

As Gordo and Hal secured the arch, Miranda went on to the next project. She filled all the metal pails with water. Then she snipped the stems on some roses from her mother's garden and floated the flowers in the pails. The buckets looked really pretty, Lizzie thought, *almost* worth Kate's snarky comment.

That afternoon, Lizzie was the last one to leave the gym. As she put on her slicker she noticed a white piece of paper by the bleachers. Curious, she picked it up. It was Hal Walters's class schedule. It must have fallen out of his pack. She tucked it safely into her own pack. She would have to remember to give it back to him.

Lizzie managed to get all her homework done by eight thirty. So when she sank into her favorite spot on the couch, she was looking forward to a well-deserved stretch of channel surfing.

There was only one problem. Her little

brother was standing directly in front of the television set. Even worse, he was wearing bizarre plaid pants and holding a golf club.

Lizzie decided to be polite. "Rat-face, would you please move?"

"Can't," Matt replied. "And silence, please. You're ruining my concentration."

That's when Lizzie noticed that the living room floor had been completely covered with bright green Astroturf.

There's something very wrong with this picture.

She shot to her feet. "What do you think you're doing?" she demanded.

"What does it look like?" Matt asked, in his I'm-so-innocent voice. He bent down and set a golf ball on a little wooden tee that was sticking out of the fake grass. Then he straightened, wound up for a swing, and hit the golf ball into the next room.

When he took a second golf ball from the pocket of those horrible plaid pants, Lizzie knew she had to take action. "Mom! Dad!" she screamed. "Could you come in here? Like, now!"

Mr. McGuire came into the living room, holding the newspaper he had been reading. "What's the problem, Lizzie?" he asked.

Lizzie pointed toward her little brother. "Matt's playing golf in the house," she said, sure her brother would get in trouble. "And he's wearing those gross plaid pants," she couldn't help adding.

"They're not plaid, they're madras," Matt informed her huffily.

"Okay, why exactly are you playing golf in the house?" Mr. McGuire wanted to know.

"Because with all this rain I haven't been able to go outside for the last two and a half weeks, and it's driving me crazy," Matt explained. "So I decided to bring the outdoors in and play a little miniature golf."

Mr. McGuire rubbed his chin. "You know, that's kind of ingenious."

"It is not!" Lizzie said. "I can't watch TV because Matt's madras-clad butt is in the way. Does he have to tee off directly in front of the TV?"

But Mr. McGuire didn't answer. He walked over to Matt and held out his hand. "Mind if I give it a try?" he asked. Matt handed his father a golf club and shot a wicked grin at Lizzie.

Arrrghh!

Ever since Gordo had told her that guys liked to be asked out, Lizzie had thought of little else. On Wednesday, as Lizzie headed toward the cafeteria, she decided to ask Ethan to be part of the Flower Power posse. She would sound confident. She would sound casual. It would be no biggie.

He'll be like putty in my hands. Right? Right!?!

Still, her stomach was doing backflips, and she was in a state of hyperalertness. She had to make sure she saw Ethan before he saw her.

It must have been that hyperalert state that made Lizzie notice something out of the corner of her eye as she passed the art room. She came to a stop, not quite believing what she'd seen. Then she tiptoed back to the art room and took a quick glance inside.

This is a professional detective technique called "sneak and peek." It looks a little silly, but trust me, all the major crime busters use it.

She hadn't imagined it. The room was empty except for Hal. He was standing at an easel, putting the finishing touches on a painting.

There wasn't anything strange about that.

Except that Lizzie had seen Hal's schedule. She pulled it out of her own pack and checked it again. Hal wasn't taking art.

"Dude."

Lizzie spun around at the sound of her crush-boy's voice. Ethan gave her a quick nod as he passed. She watched as he walked to the cafeteria.

Lizzie summoned her courage again. It didn't seem to be responding.

"Oh, courage . . . yoo-hoo, courage . . . where are you?"

She followed Ethan to his table, anyway. At least he was by himself. Which meant she'd only be humiliating herself in front of one person.

"Hey, dude, what's up?" Ethan asked. He was about to bite into a humongous sandwich.

"Um . . . Ethan, I was wondering." Lizzie

hesitated, then blurted it all out in a rush. "Do you want to join the Flower Power posse?"

Ethan looked at her blankly, and Lizzie cringed. She couldn't even believe she had said that aloud.

"Uh, what's the Flower Power posse?"

"We're getting the gym ready for Spring Fling," Lizzie explained. "You know—putting up lights and flowers and stuff."

There was an extremely long moment in which Ethan furrowed his brow and seemed to consider this. Finally, he looked at Lizzie and said, "Sorry, dude. Flowers aren't my thing."

Lizzie mumbled, "No worries, that's cool," and turned to flee—only to have someone grab her elbow.

It was Miranda, and she looked upset. "I need you in the gym now. Emergency meeting. We've got trouble—big-time!"

The Flower Power posse stood in the gym, trying to make sense of what they saw. The metal buckets with floating flowers had been emptied and stacked together. The roses had been stuffed in the trash, and a moldy mop stuck out of the top bucket. Ew!

And the tiny white Christmas lights had been replaced with strands of red chili-pepper lights. The white lights were gone. Luckily, the arch was still standing.

"This is extremely strange," Gordo said.

"Strange? It's a disaster!" Miranda moaned. "This is Spring Fling, not a chili cook-off."

"I think the chili-pepper lights are kind of cute," Jolie said. "They're festive. And red."

Hal just stared at the chili-pepper lights with an unreadable expression.

"Kate did this," Miranda fumed. "And I'm going to get her back."

"Slow down," Gordo advised. "Stealing lights—and taking the trouble to put up new ones—isn't exactly Kate's style. You can't prove she did it, can you?"

"Not yet," Miranda admitted. "But I bet Lizzie will."

Lizzie wasn't sure how she felt about this vote of confidence. This latest incident only seemed to make things more confusing.

"How about Mr. Zaber?" Jolie asked. "After all, he would have known how to set off the sprinkler system. And he could change the lights, no problem."

"What's his motive?" Lizzie asked. She knew a culprit always had to have a motive.

"He wasn't happy about us messing with his clean gym," Jolie said at once. "And when he saw the little white lights, he must have realized that we borrowed his ladder again. What we're looking at is payback."

In spite of herself, Lizzie was impressed with Jolie's reasoning.

"One more thing," Jolie added, "we've got a major piece of evidence. The mop points to him for sure."

7

Lizzie jotted down Jolie's theories in her note-book. She began trying to add it all up. "Everyone knows Mr. Zaber is cranky," she said. "And we know he thinks we're a nuisance."

"That's for sure," Hal agreed.

"I can imagine him trashing the roses, and stacking the buckets, and even ripping down the Christmas lights," Lizzie went on. "But *putting* up chili lights? It just doesn't fit."

"Maybe he wants the principal to cancel the dance," Jolie suggested. "Or maybe Mr. Zaber has some secret he's hiding and that's why he doesn't want us in the gym."

"That doesn't make sense," Lizzie objected. "The whole school uses the gym."

"Not this week," Gordo reminded her.

The bell for the next period rang. "I'm sorry, guys," Miranda said. "We didn't get to eat lunch because of this."

"It's okay," Lizzie said. She was still relieved that Miranda had saved her from more humiliation with Ethan.

"Wait a minute." Jolie planted herself in front of Lizzie. "You're making a list of suspects, right?"

Lizzie nodded.

"Are you going to add Mr. Zaber?" Jolie asked.

Lizzie shut her notebook. "He's already on it."

Now probably isn't the time to tell her that she's on the list, too.

* * *

Lizzie headed to her locker to get her books for the final class of the day. She stopped as she saw Miranda, Jolie, Gordo, and Hal, all gathered near Miranda's open locker. Miranda caught Lizzie's eye and waved her over.

"Quick update," Miranda said. "The good news is, Principal Tweedy gave us permission to borrow Mr. Zaber's ladder and take down the chili lights. The bad news is that we can't meet in the gym this afternoon because Mr. Zaber's waxing the floor."

Hal reached out and almost absentmindedly switched the positions of two rock-star photos that Miranda had stuck to the inside of her locker door with magnets, so that the larger one was on top. It looked better that way, Lizzie realized. "Listen," he said, "I can come in early tomorrow and take down the lights before school starts."

"And I can come help him!" Jolie said brightly.

Could she be any more obvious?

Lizzie smiled at Jolie. "I'll come, too," she said.

"But you never get to school early," Gordo protested.

Lizzie poked him in the ribs. "This is important," she said. What she meant was, Hal and Jolie were both suspects. And if they were the culprits, she wanted to make sure that neither one would get a chance to undo anything else.

That evening Lizzie trudged toward the stairs to her bedroom, her mood glum. Miranda had never said she was counting on Lizzie to solve the mystery, but Lizzie knew it was up to her. She had to find the saboteur before the dance was totally ruined. She decided to go over the list of suspects again. Jolie was a suspect because she was competing with Miranda and had access to the school Web site. Mr. Zaber was a suspect because he had motive and access. And though it was hard to imagine that Hal was the culprit— he'd put so much work into decking out the gym—there was something strange about him not taking art class but painting in the art room. Plus, he hadn't seemed very upset by any of the disasters. Still, none of them felt quite right. Lizzie thought back to the she-beast's remarks in the auditorium. Kate had just about promised that the dance would be a disaster.

Maybe it's time I focused my investigation on the source of everything evil at Hillridge.

Lizzie was so deep in thought that she didn't even hear Matt yell, "It's going all the way downtown!

"Look out, it's a bomb!" he yelled.

She turned and saw a golf ball soaring straight at her. She ducked as it whizzed over her head, thunked down behind her, and rolled to a stop at the foot of the stairs.

"Mom!" Lizzie got to her feet, shrieking. "Make him stop!"

The little cretin, in his eyesore-plaid pants, was teeing off again. "Just be the ball," he muttered to himself. "Just be the ball."

"And he's speaking gibberish!" Lizzie added helpfully.

"It's launched—and it's large!" Matt exclaimed as his club hit the ball and launched it like a missile. There was a moment of silence—then a loud shattering sound as the golf ball connected with Mrs. McGuire's favorite crystal vase.

Mrs. McGuire came into the room, hands on hips. "What was that?"

Neither Matt nor Lizzie answered.

Mrs. McGuire's jaw dropped as she spotted the remains of her crystal vase. Lizzie could see her mom silently counting to ten so she wouldn't lose her temper.

When she finally spoke, Mrs. McGuire's voice was perfectly calm. "Matt, you are going to clean up the pieces of my vase. Sweep and then vacuum. I don't want to find a single sliver anywhere."

"It was just a flub," Matt started to explain. "I—"

"Then you are going to take apart the golf course," their mother continued in the same cool tone. "I want the golf clubs, the ball, the Astroturf, all of it in the garage within the hour. Do you understand me?"

And lose the plaid pants while you're at it!

"But, Mom," Matt pleaded, "I was just starting to get off some really fine shots. If that one hadn't connected with the vase, it would have been killer—flame-broiled!"

Mrs. McGuire's eyes widened behind her glasses. "If you don't clean that up immediately, I'm going to flame-broil your golf gear!"

"Okay, okay." Matt headed toward the broom closet. "You don't have to get so crabby about it."

Lizzie felt bad. She knew that her mom had loved that crystal vase. But as for the end of the living-room golf course? Lizzie decided it was the first thing that had gone right all week.

CHAPTER

8

On Thursday morning, forty-five minutes before the first bell rang, Lizzie squooshed into school in her new rain boots. Somehow she had managed to get water inside them. Her socks were already spongy and drenched, her toes cold.

Even though she was—for Lizzie—at school ridiculously early, she was late for the early-morning posse meeting. Hal and Jolie were already in the gym, but they weren't taking down the chili lights. Hal was kneeling on the floor, unwrapping what looked like a large wet sheet. Jolie knelt by his side.

This was definitely suspicious. "What have you got there?" Lizzie asked.

Please don't tell me it's a body.

"Look." Hal lifted the last layer of sheet. Inside it was a thick bunch of long, feathery green plants.

"Ferns?" Lizzie asked.

Jolie looked up at her. "Do you think Fern is a pretty name?" she asked. "Because I was thinking that when I'm sixteen I might change my name to Fern. Or maybe Danielle. Danielle's one of my favorite names, too." She scrunched up her face in concentration. "Actually, I think Danielle's prettier than Fern."

Lizzie blinked. She didn't even want to try to

follow that one. "Where did the ferns come from?" she asked Hal.

"I borrowed them from the park," he explained.

"Why?" Lizzie asked. "What are they for?"

Hal smiled and said, "Swags. Watch." He took a few of the long fronds and began weaving them together into a long green rope. "We can wrap these across the arch."

"Cool," Lizzie said, impressed. "Uh, Hal, I found your schedule the other day."

She took Hal's class schedule from her pack and handed it to him.

"Thanks." He stuck it in his pocket without glancing at it, then grabbed two of the buckets. "I'm going to put some water in these, so we can keep the ferns from wilting. Then let's get rid of these chili lights." Hal walked back to the boys' locker room, leaving Lizzie alone with Jolie.

Jolie pulled her handheld computer from her pack and began tapping on its keyboard. It suddenly occurred to Lizzie that if Jolie was their saboteur, the evidence might be on her pocket computer.

"Jolie," Lizzie said. "I—uh—was wondering about the weather for tomorrow. Can you check the weather on that?"

"Duh," Jolie said. "It's going to rain. Who needs to check a computer? But yeah, I'll double-check."

She tapped some more keys. "Rain, for sure," she announced.

"Could I see?" Lizzie needed Jolie to hand over the minicomputer so Lizzie could have a quick look at her files.

Well, you never know. She might just have a file called Nefarious Plans to Ruin Spring Fling!

"Sure." Jolie held the little computer out to

Lizzie, then snatched it back at the last second. "Wait, there's something I've got to show you. It's the best site."

Seconds later Lizzie was looking at the tiny screen, trying to make out the even tinier lettering. "Something about small furry things?"

"Exactly! It's the coolest—the baby animals site. They have like a million photos of puppies and kittens and baby bunnies and seals, and they're all totally adorable. Look at this baby mongoose. Can you believe it?"

"Scroll to the weasel family," Jolie suggested as she went to help Hal.

As if I didn't already have a little weasel in the family.

Lizzie quickly called up a directory of Jolie's files, and began skimming their names: Perfect Pups, Kitten Capers, Lip Gloss, Bunnies Galore,

Lovable Lemurs, Fruit-Scented Hair Condition-ers . . . Lizzie opened a few. The animal files all showed dozens of photos of animals. The conditioner and lip gloss files were collections of downloaded ads. Lizzie couldn't take anymore. If Jolie was making evil plans, they weren't on her handheld.

Meanwhile, Hal was sliding the buckets of ferns underneath the tall end of the bleachers. "That should keep them from being knocked over," he said.

They went to work on the lights next. Five minutes later, they had taken down all of the chili lights. They were folding the strands into a plastic bag when the gym door opened and Kate stuck her head in.

"What do you want?" Lizzie asked.

"Nothing to do with you," Kate assured her. "I just wanted to see what Hal was up to."

"I'm taking down lights," Hal answered. "Satisfied?"

"Totally." Kate flashed him her perfect smile and left.

The gears in Lizzie's brain started to whir. Hmm, what did the she-beast want with Hal? . . .

To Lizzie's surprise, Jolie asked the million-dollar question. "Hal, how come Kate Sanders is checking up on you?"

"Because she's Kate," he replied tersely.

"And?" Lizzie asked.

Hal looked up at the clock on the gym wall. "And first bell's going to ring and I've got to get to my locker."

Hal's cell phone rang then. He frowned at the digital display, then flipped it open. "What? No, I can't tomorrow." He sounded annoyed. "Fine, then I will." He snapped it closed. He looked more than annoyed, Lizzie thought, he looked angry. "Later," he said, and started out of the gym.

"I'll walk you," Jolie offered, and hurried out after him.

Lizzie stayed and whipped out her detective notebook, scrawling: who called Hal and what do they want him to do tomorrow? What if it was Kate and she's using Hal to spy on us and give her information? What if Kate and Hal have teamed up to sabotage Spring Fling?

Lizzie strode into the cafeteria at lunchtime, determined to check out the Hal-Kate connection. She had no idea of how, but she knew that she'd think of something.

All great detectives are cunning, resourceful, and inventive, not to mention very slick. So I have a plan: I am going to outslick Kate.

There was only one problem with that plan. Kate was nowhere in sight. Before she could look somewhere else, she heard her name being called.

"Lizzie, over here!" Miranda was waving to her from a table near the back of the room where she was sitting with Gordo.

Her investigation temporarily stalled, Lizzie went to eat lunch with her friends. Gordo was reporting on his sociology study when she got there.

"Best dating method so far," Gordo said, "is to go shopping together."

"For clothes?" Miranda asked, surprised.

"Nope, that's a complete disaster," Gordo replied. "Guys do not want to wait around while a girl tries on twenty T-shirts and asks if each one makes her look fat. What works is shopping together for CDs or DVDs."

"Guys, guys!" Jolie raced up to the table, wild-eyed. "There you are! I've been looking all over the school for you."

"Why?" Miranda asked.

"When we were taking down the lights this

morning, my lip gloss fell out of my purse," she explained. "And I just went down to get it and, Miranda, someone's taken down the arch! It's in little pieces all over the floor!"

Miranda went pale. "I put a deposit down on that arch with my own money," she said. "Now, not only will I not get my money back, but I'm going to have to pay full price for whatever that arch costs." She put her head down on the table. "I give up," she said. "Kate was right. Flower Power just wilted. We've got to tell Principal Tweedy to cancel the dance."

"Miranda, you can't give up!" Lizzie said at once. "That's exactly what Kate—or whoever's been sabotaging us—wants."

"Lizzie's right," Gordo added. "If we give up, the saboteur wins."

"And," Jolie chimed in, "I went online last night and bought a vintage flower-print dress to wear to the dance, and it's not returnable!"

"Besides," Gordo said, "you've got a delivery of flowers coming from the garden store this afternoon. We've got to figure out where they go."

"We'll make it work," Lizzie promised her friend. "I'm not sure how, but we'll make this the best Spring Fling ever!"

That afternoon, after school let out, the Flower Power posse once again gathered in the gym. Gordo swept up the pieces of the arch.

"Could I see one of those pieces?" Lizzie asked.

Gordo handed her one of the broken pieces, and Lizzie examined it carefully. "How do you think this happened?" she asked. "A saw?"

Gordo ran his finger along a broken edge. "Nope, if it was cut with a saw, you'd see jagged teeth marks. This looks a little twisted and cut. Like someone took tin snips to it."

"Where would someone in this school get tin snips?" Lizzie asked.

"Mr. Zaber probably has a pair somewhere," Gordo said. "And I have a pair, in the toolbox in my locker."

"I think we need to see if the ones in your toolbox are missing," Lizzie said.

Gordo nodded. They made a quick trip to his locker, retrieved the toolbox, and brought it back to the gym. Gordo opened the toolbox. There on the top shelf were the tin snips. "Right where I left them," he said.

Lizzie sighed. "That points us back to Mr. Zaber."

"Of course. He's the main suspect," said Jolie.

And let's not forget about you. . . .

Hal dragged one of the big metal stands that held up the volleyball net to one side of the door, then went to get the other one.

"What are you doing?" Miranda asked.

He flashed her a pure-charm smile. "You'll see. Just trust me."

"Look," he said. "We just lift the net, and attach it on either end, so it drapes across the top of the two poles, kind of like a hammock," Hal explained.

Miranda looked baffled. "Then what?"

"We add ferns," Hal answered. He darted behind the bleachers and returned with the two buckets filled with ferns. As Miranda watched, astonished, Hal climbed up Gordo's stepladder and draped the ferns across the net, his fingers working deftly. Next, using twine to secure them, he wrapped the remaining ferns around the metal poles.

Finally, he turned toward Miranda and bowed. "A green entryway to your garden, mademoiselle."

Miranda gave a little hop of excitement. "I love it!"

"It will look even better when we thread some flowers through the top and along the poles," Hal promised.

A knock sounded against the gym door. Miranda pushed it open and found the delivery guy from the garden store. "I have flats of pansies and snapdragons," the man said. "Is this the right place?"

"This is it," Miranda said.

Moments later, flats of flowers sat on the gym floor.

"Hmm . . ." Jolie said. "These don't look like the kinds of flowers you can put in vases."

"That's true," Miranda admitted. "They're not cut flowers. They're much cheaper. I thought we could figure some cool way to disguise the plastic containers and then set them on the floor, like the edging on garden paths."

Gordo looked doubtful. "Won't people step on them if they're on the floor?"

"I want garden paths." Miranda crossed her arms over her chest. "I couldn't get lilacs, my Japanese lanterns are trashed, and so is my arch. I'm not giving up on garden paths."

"Well, maybe we can figure out something else for that," Hal said. He picked up one of the containers of pansies. "I think Gordo's right. These are gonna get crushed on the floor. What if we set them on top of the bleachers, like window boxes?"

"That's not a bad idea," Miranda allowed. "We could wrap thick ribbon around the plastic containers, like sashes."

"Except you wouldn't really see that if you were down on the floor dancing," Gordo pointed out. "We need something flashier."

"Colored foil!" Hal suggested. "We could use spring colors—purples and pinks and greens."

"And reds!" Jolie piped up.

Miranda frowned. "Okay, we'll go with the foil, then."

Lizzie looked at her watch. "It's getting late," she said. "We should figure out what to do with these flowers for now. We shouldn't leave them in the gym—just in case the saboteur strikes again."

"Why don't we put them in Mr. Pettus's room?" Gordo suggested.

Mr. Pettus was one of the eighth-grade science teachers. His room was part laboratory, so it was bigger than most classrooms.

They all carried flats of flowers up to the science room. Lizzie turned on the lights and heard squeaking sounds. One lab table was covered with tanks and cages. Mr. Pettus had all sorts of animals for observation—four guinea pigs, two rabbits, two toads, and a garden snake named Truman.

"Oh, they're all so cute!" Jolie said. She turned to the guinea pigs. "Is it okay with you guys if we leave the flowers here overnight?"

"They say yes," Gordo answered quickly. "Let's go."

They set the flowers on the floor behind one of the big lab tables.

"There." Miranda seemed satisfied. "I'll come to school early tomorrow and ask Mr. P if we can just leave them here until the dance."

CHAPTER

10

Miranda was one of the first people Lizzie saw when she got to school on Friday. She was leaning against her locker, with a troubled expression.

"What's up?" Lizzie asked.

"I forgot a detail that is majorly *important*," Miranda said.

"Which is?"

"Did you ever ask Ethan to Spring Fling?"

Lizzie winced. "Please. Let's not go there."

"Okay, here's the problem," Miranda said. "I've been so busy worrying about decorating the gym, I totally forgot about actually going to the dance. We've got a situation, *chica*. We are dateless for our own dance, which is exactly one day away! This calls for desperate measures."

"Not *Star Wars* trivia contests!" Lizzie pleaded.

Miranda grinned. "We're not *that* desperate. But I think we should be brave and tough it out. I'll ask Hal if you'll ask Ethan."

Lizzie thought about it. She thought about being turned down three times. But she also knew she couldn't quite give up her dream of going to Spring Fling with Ethan Craft. "Okay," she agreed. "I'll ask if you will."

Miranda glanced at her watch. "Hey, we've still got ten minutes before homeroom. Let's go water the flowers in Mr. Pettus's room."

The two girls stepped into the science lab. "No, Mr. Pettus," Lizzie observed. "I guess he hasn't come in yet. What are we going to use for a watering can?"

Miranda set her books on one of the high lab

tables and picked up a plastic beaker. "This will work," she said, and filled it in the lab sink.

Lizzie grabbed another plastic beaker as Miranda walked around the table to begin watering. Miranda stopped suddenly. "Not again!" she wailed.

Lizzie bolted over to where Miranda stood, and a sick, sinking feeling settled in her stomach. The flats of flowers had been overturned. Dirt and stems littered the floor.

"I can't believe it," Lizzie said. "The flowers are all gone."

"What flowers?"

Lizzie whirled around to see Mr. Pettus in the doorway of his classroom, looking very confused.

Miranda was seething. "All those innocent little flowers beheaded. This is pure evil," she said. "Who would do such a thing?"

Lizzie spotted the culprits and sighed. "I know exactly who did this." She pointed to Herbert and Clementine, the science room bunnies, who were happily munching on the last of the pansies.

Mr. Pettus joined them on the other side of the lab table and surveyed the damage. "I think," he said, "that you two have a bit of explaining to do."

Lizzie and Miranda told him they'd left the flowers in the science room the night before.

"We can't explain," Lizzie concluded, "how the rabbits got out of their cage. They were definitely in it yesterday when we left the flowers here."

Mr. Pettus rubbed his forehead. "I can't explain it, either. I check the locks on the cages every day before I leave." He glanced up at the clock. "The homeroom bell is going to ring any minute now. I'll round up the rabbits if you two could sweep up. I'll give you passes if you're late."

"Sure, no problem," Lizzie said. "We just have to go get a broom and dustpan. We'll be right back." And before Miranda could argue, Lizzie grabbed her by the arm and hustled her out of the science room.

"Why are you so keen on sweeping up?"

Miranda asked once they were in the hallway.

"Because this is exactly the opportunity we need," Lizzie said. "We've got to get to the bottom of this mystery, and I think Mr. Zaber is our first stop."

"Ulp!" Miranda said.

"I know, he's grouchy," Lizzie agreed. "But we can't let that scare us. We've got to make sure that he is not the one sabotaging the dance."

A few minutes later, Lizzie and Miranda stood in the janitor's office. "We need to borrow a broom and a dustpan," Lizzie explained. "To clean up the science room."

Mr. Zaber rolled his eyes. "Now what happened?"

As if you didn't know, Lizzie thought. But she explained that someone unlocked the cage in Mr. Pettus's room, and the bunnies had eaten all the flowers that were on the floor.

"And why were there flowers on the floor?" Mr. Zaber asked.

Lizzie decided to play along.

Time to smoke him out. Or trip him up. Or something they do on all the cop shows.

So she began to explain why they had taken the flowers to the science room. And Miranda, who hopefully understood what she was doing, joined in.

"Mr. Pettus's room seemed the safest place for them," Miranda concluded.

"What we can't figure out," Lizzie said innocently, "is who could have let two bunnies out of a locked cage. I mean, besides Mr. Pettus, who has the key?"

"I do," Mr. Zaber snapped. "I have keys to every lock in this school."

Bingo! Lizzie was elated. She could skip the rest of junior high, high school, and even college—and go straight to work as chief detective. Every police department in the country was going to want someone with her skill at interrogating suspects and cracking cases!

All suspects quake in their shoes when McGuire runs the investigation. Except maybe Mr. Zaber.

"But I never go into the science room," Mr. Zaber went on. "I'm allergic to fur, so I have to get Mr. Norris, the part-time janitor, to clean it."

"Aha!" Lizzie cried. "So Mr. Norris opened the cage."

"Mr. Norris wasn't here yesterday," said Mr. Zaber. "He called in sick."

A good detective knows when a lead goes *splah*. Time to change the subject.

"Okay," Lizzie said. "How about the sprinklers? You blamed us for those going off, but on Saturday we left the school before you did."

The janitor was quiet for a long moment. "I should have told you. I figured out the problem on Monday afternoon. I even told the principal. There was a crack in one of the valves." He frowned at them. "But don't expect any apologies. You kids still made a mess."

Mr. Zaber handed them brooms and dustpans. "Now go clean up Mr. Pettus's floor."

Lizzie and Miranda made their way back up to the science room.

"Okay, that was a bust," Miranda said. "I have a feeling that Mr. Zaber should come off the list."

"Yeah," Lizzie agreed. "At least there's one good thing. We've eliminated a suspect. So that means now it can only be Jolie or Kate or Hal."

11

Lizzie's stomach was in knots when she entered the cafeteria on Friday afternoon. If she was going to ask Ethan to the dance, it was now or never. She imagined all the ways that he could turn her down:

"Me, go to the dance with you? Are you serious?"

"No way, dude. I've got a highly important TV rerun I've got to watch."

"Why would I want to do that?"

"Thanks, but I'd really rather pick fleas off my dog."

This is actually a sophisticated psychological strategy: imagine the worst and then whatever happens seems better. Will it work? Who knows? I just made it up.

Lizzie took a deep breath and gazed around the crowded cafeteria, looking for Ethan. Even if her hair was frizzed from the rain, at least she was wearing her favorite pink stretchy top.

Hmmm . . . no Ethan in sight. But she spied Kate and Hal talking intently. What exactly was going on between them? The weird thing was, it didn't look like they were crushing on each other. It looked as if they were arguing.

Lizzie knew she had to check it out. She had to figure out what the Hal-Kate connection really was.

Talk about slick . . . I am about to pull the slickest move of my detecting career.

Very, very casually, Lizzie turned her back to them. Then slowly but deliberately she began to inch backward toward Hal and Kate. She edged closer and closer until she was almost within eavesdropping distance. She could hear their voices now, but in the din of the cafeteria she couldn't make out their exact words.

Totally nonchalant, she took another step backward.

"McGuire!" Kate snapped. "What are you doing? You're about to—"

But Kate's warning came too late. Lizzie collided with Larry Tudgeman's lunch tray. Tudgeman's chocolate pudding whooshed up into the air and came down *splat!*—all over Lizzie and Tudgeman.

Lizzie felt cool chocolate pudding drip down her face and seep into her pink stretchy top.

Kate pointed at her then nearly collapsed in gales of laughter. "Oh, McGuire," she gasped. "This is your best yet. Could you get any dorkier?"

"I was really looking forward to eating that pudding," Tudgeman said.

"I'm really sorry," Lizzie told him and fled toward the girls' room.

A glance in the mirror made her moan. What a disaster! Her favorite pink stretchy top was now coated with giant chocolate splotches. Lizzie grabbed a handful of paper towels, held them under the sink, and tried to clean off the chocolate pudding. This was *so* not how she wanted things to work out.

That afternoon, Lizzie, Gordo, and Miranda were the only members of the posse to meet in the gym. Lizzie was wearing a white lab coat, which she had begged Mr. Pettus to lend her. It totally covered the pudding stains, and Lizzie kind of liked it. It sort of made her look like one of those glamorous but intense interns on her favorite TV hospital show. She could just imagine herself slinging a stethoscope around her neck and saying, "Get me an EKC, stat!"

Or is it ECT? EKP?? EGZ???

"So, did you invite Hal to Spring Fling?" Gordo asked Miranda.

Miranda shrugged, looking slightly embarrassed. "Yeah, but he told me Jolie already asked him, and he said yes." She shook her head. "How could Hal fall for Jolie?"

"Maybe he was just flattered to have a girl ask

him out," Gordo suggested. "We fall for that sometimes. It's a guy thing."

Lizzie emerged from her doctor daydream, and said, "Miranda, there's something you should know about Hal. He and Kate know each other."

"So?" Miranda asked.

"I mean, I think they know each other really well," Lizzie explained. "I saw them talking today, and it was really intense."

"But he's going to the dance with Jolie." Miranda sounded confused.

"I don't think Hal's exactly crushing on Kate," Lizzie said. "It's something else. . . ."

"Like what?" Gordo asked.

Lizzie looked around the gym and thought of all the things that had gone wrong so far. "I think Hal and Kate may be working together to ruin Spring Fling."

"That doesn't make sense," Gordo argued. "Hal's the one who's had most of the ideas we used. Why would he want to wreck them?"

"Besides," Miranda added, "you said that Hal doesn't have access to the student Web site."

"But Kate does," Lizzie reminded her. "And if they're working together—"

"What about Jolie?" Miranda asked.

"Jolie doesn't exactly strike me as the criminal type," Gordo said. "She's too flaky to be a saboteur."

Miranda looked inspired. "Maybe Jolie and Kate are working together!"

"Doubtful," Lizzie said. "Jolie doesn't hang with Kate's coven. I don't think she's mean enough. Right now Hal is at the top of my list."

"Okay," Miranda said. "Let's all keep an eye on him. In the meantime, though, we've got to figure out a way to turn this gym into a garden. The bunnies ate all our flowers. And my budget—not counting the arch that I still haven't paid for—is now down to twenty dollars."

"Maybe we should revisit the idea of fake flowers," Gordo suggested. "I've seen some really nice silk ones."

"No." Miranda was firm. "We have to have fresh flowers. Scent is very important. Otherwise it will just smell like the gym."

Smelling like the gym-nauseum is definitely not a good thing.

"Gordo," Miranda asked, "do you think we could take some from your mother's garden?"

"Only if you want me to be grounded for the rest of my life," Gordo replied.

"Hal said he 'borrowed' the ferns from the park," Lizzie remembered. "I might have seen some daffodils there the other day."

Funny how Hal seems to have a talent for "borrowing" things.

Gordo shook his head. "People get arrested for stunts like that. I can't believe Hal got away with taking the ferns."

"My mom said I couldn't take any more flowers," Miranda said. "That only leaves us one option." Miranda looked directly at Lizzie.

"Forget it," Lizzie told them. "My mom was too busy last fall to plant bulbs. The only flowers in our yard are some scrawny dandelions.

"Wait a minute," Lizzie said. "I just got a brilliant idea. Let's all meet back here in the morning at nine."

"You're not going to tell us what this brilliant idea is?" Gordo asked.

"Can't," Lizzie said. "Not until I'm sure I can get the little rodent to agree."

On Saturday morning Lizzie got to school at eight. She opened the gym door cautiously, not wanting to find any more sabotage. The ferns that Hal had wrapped around the volleyball posts still looked really green and pretty.

Lizzie turned to her parents and Matt, who had followed her into the gym. "Let's bring it in," she said.

Occasionally we McGuires stick together.

The four of them carried rolls of fake grass into the gym. Lizzie had remembered her brother's Astroturf—it seemed perfect for garden paths. With Matt "I have the most Astroturf experience" directing, they began to lay out the paths. Mrs. McGuire even brought her own white Christmas lights, which Mr. McGuire put up.

Forty minutes later, Lizzie stood alone in the gym, waiting for her friends to show. She had a sudden awful thought: what if Miranda hates Astroturf?

The gym door opened, Miranda and Gordo came in. Miranda's jaw dropped. Then she kneeled down and touched the fake grass. "Lizzie," she said, quietly. "Where did this stuff come from?"

Lizzie grinned. "Would you believe my mutant brother donated it? And he and my parents all helped put it down."

"Yes!" Miranda stood up and did a little dance.

"We've got garden paths! And lights! Spring Fling is going to be awesome!" She threw her arms around Lizzie. "You're the best friend ever!"

I hope she remembers that if I can't solve the mystery.

"I hate to put a damper on this, but we still have the flower problem," Gordo pointed out.

Miranda nodded. "I know. I can only afford to buy a few bunches."

"We could put those in the buckets," Lizzie suggested.

"Yeah, and it will look like a few bunches of flowers stuck in buckets. It won't look like a spring garden." Miranda shrugged. "Maybe that's just the way it's gotta be." She took out her wallet. "I'm going to call around to some florists and see where we can get the cheapest flowers. We'll just work with whatever we find." Miranda set off for the pay phone.

"So," Gordo said to Lizzie when they were the only ones in the gym, "what happened yesterday when you asked Ethan to the dance?"

"I never got a chance," Lizzie admitted. "I had that run-in with Tudgeman's pudding. I didn't even see Ethan yesterday."

"Oh," Gordo said, "that's interesting. Because I think crush-boy is looking through the gym window now."

Lizzie glanced over her shoulder and gasped. Gordo was right!

"Talk to him," Gordo said, taking her by the shoulders and turning her toward the door.

Lizzie stumbled toward the door and came to a halt. Her brain was frozen. She didn't have the first idea of what to do or say.

Behind her, Gordo gave an exasperated sigh. "If you want to talk to him, it might help if you didn't have a door between you." When Lizzie remained frozen in place, he opened the gym door. "Hey, Ethan," he said. "Come on in."

"Dude," Ethan said. Lizzie wasn't sure if he meant her or Gordo.

"Hi," she finally managed to get out. "Um. What are you doing here?"

"My little sister," Ethan said. "She takes the Saturday drama class here. I just dropped her off in the auditorium. My stepmom will pick her up later."

"Oh," Lizzie said.

"This is promising," Gordo whispered in her ear. "He just strung four sentences together."

Lizzie elbowed Gordo in the stomach and took a step forward. A step closer to the gorgeous Ethan. His eyes were so blue, his hair perfectly sun-streaked—

"So what's going on in here?" Ethan asked, looking around the gym. "Astroturf, cool! You going to play miniature golf?"

"No golf," Lizzie said. "We're decorating the gym for tonight's Spring Fling dance."

Gordo was whispering in Lizzie's ear again. "Now! Ask him!"

This time Lizzie stepped on Gordo's toe.

When she was sure Gordo had retreated a safe distance away, she said, "Uh, Ethan, are you going to the dance tonight?"

"Looks that way," Ethan answered. "Maybe I'll see you there?"

Okay, that wasn't exactly "Will you go to the dance with me?" but it's probably as close as I'm going to get.

Lizzie wanted to shriek, "Yes, I'll definitely be there and I'd love to dance with you!" But she knew she had to play it cool. This was Ethan, after all.

"Maybe," she finally replied, hoping she sounded supercasual.

"You mean, you might not go?" Ethan asked.

Lizzie realized she had confused him. "No, I'm definitely going," she said.

"Oh." Ethan looked around the gym again. "So where are all the flowers?"

"That's the problem," Lizzie admitted. She gave a brief account of all the mishaps they had suffered.

"Oh," Ethan said again, though he looked almost thoughtful this time.

The gym door opened and Miranda walked back in. She didn't even notice the miracle of Ethan standing there talking to Lizzie. Her shoulders slumped and her eyes were glued to the floor.

"No good," she reported. "With my remaining twenty bucks I can buy two bunches of mixed flowers and one pot of geraniums."

Lizzie wrinkled her nose. "Geraniums don't really smell all that great."

The gym door opened again. This time, Hal and Jolie came in.

"Sorry I didn't show yesterday," Hal said. "I got

summoned for a family thing. Parental orders."

"And I had to go to the dentist," Jolie explained.

Hal seemed to notice the Astroturf and the lights for the first time. He nodded, a smile lighting his face. "It's got potential," he said. "All we need now are some flowers."

"Where are the pansies and snapdragons?" Jolie asked.

"Eaten by bunnies," Miranda told her.

A strange look flashed between Jolie and Hal, but it was over so quickly, Lizzie wasn't sure what she'd just seen.

Miranda sighed. "Never mind. I think I just have to buy a lot more crepe paper. We can't afford real flowers."

"I can get you flowers," Ethan said.

"What?" Gordo, Lizzie, and Miranda all spoke at the same time.

Ethan shrugged. "My aunt Valerie is a florist. She does a lot of weddings and parties. She's got a shop about ten miles from here, and she always has leftover flowers, the ones that aren't perfect enough for the arrangements."

Miranda looked as if she were trying not to be too hopeful. "Can we call her and ask if she has any we could use?"

"Sure." Ethan flipped his cell phone open and punched in a number. He had a brief conversation, then flipped it closed. "Aunt Valerie said she's got plenty of extras, and we should just come take what we want. The number five bus goes there."

Miranda gave a little shriek of joy. "Thank you!"

Lizzie was very glad the flower situation was going to work out. But she was even happier about something else: she might get to sit next to Ethan on the bus!

The number five crosstown bus was overheated and crowded and smelled like damp socks, but Lizzie couldn't have been happier. She and Ethan were actually doing something together, and it didn't feel weird or awkward. Of course, they were there with four friends and a busload of strangers, but why be picky?

Ethan hadn't actually said anything to her since they got on the bus. Then he turned to her and said, "Do you have change for a dollar?"

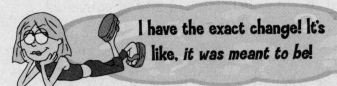

I have the exact change! It's like, *it was meant to be!*

Hmm, Lizzie thought. What can I say that will completely dazzle Ethan and get him to fall in love with me?

Thinking, thinking. It just needs to be something totally cool and memorable.

As Lizzie pondered the perfect opening to a conversation with crush-boy, Hal's cell phone rang. Lizzie watched as he had a brisk, short conversation. It ended with him saying, "I'm going to a flower shop, okay? No, I don't know when I'll be back."

He flipped the phone closed, and Lizzie noticed he looked upset. One thing she was sure of: Hal hadn't wanted to talk to whoever called. Which made Lizzie want to know who that person was.

Deciding a direct approach was best, she leaned forward to ask Hal who his mysterious caller was. At that exact moment, Ethan decided to strike up a conversation with her.

"So, dude, it's really raining, huh?" Ethan began.

The moment of truth every top detective eventually faces: pursue my investigation or pursue romance? Quick answer: crush-boy wins.

Lizzie sat back in her seat and thought for a moment. "Yeah," she said, smiling. "It is."

The bus dropped Lizzie and her friends in front of a small but charming house. The sign on the lawn read, VALERIE'S FLOWERS. Ethan led the way up onto the porch and rang the doorbell. Lizzie gazed at him adoringly. Her crush-boy was rescuing Spring Fling! How heroic was that?

A small woman with a long, dark ponytail answered the door. She wore jeans and a flannel shirt, and she had a smudge of yellow pollen on her nose. Lizzie liked her at once.

Valerie smiled at the group on the porch, then

reached up and hugged Ethan. "Come on in, everyone," she said. "Want a quick tour of my workroom?"

Valerie led them to a glass-enclosed room on the side of the house. The most beautiful flowers Lizzie had ever seen covered every surface. The room was filled with just about every color imaginable—purples and reds and yellows, bright blues and oranges, gentle lavenders and whites. Suddenly, Lizzie understood what Miranda had been working toward all along. Flowers were beyond bling-bling—they were magic!

"So my extras," Valerie was saying, "are in the potting shed in the backyard. They're not quite this quality, but I think you'll find things you can use. And there baskets and vases back there—so help yourselves."

"This is the answer to my dreams!" Miranda told Ethan's aunt.

Lizzie and her friend trooped across the rainy yard to the potting shed. It was a long, low, wooden building that smelled of the bags of potting soil piled against the walls and the flowers lying on the rough wooden table. Miranda looked around, took a deep breath, and said, "Let's just make the most beautiful arrangements we can, and then we'll find places for them in the gym."

Lizzie picked up some tiger lilies and irises. *Plop!* She looked up. The shed's roof was leaking!

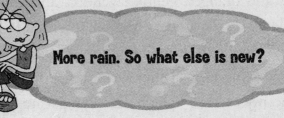

More rain. So what else is new?

Lizzie sighed and kept working. Everyone—except Ethan—was totally involved in making flower creations. Ethan cheered them on, though, even declaring one of Lizzie's arrangements "radical." Lizzie felt positively soggy and weirdly happy. But all the time she was trying to do something artistic with flowers, she was also watching Hal. Was he their saboteur?

It was hard to believe. Hal was working harder than any of them, turning out one gorgeous arrangement after another. And yet Lizzie's gut told her he was the culprit. She had to confront him. But not until they got the flowers together!

Two hours later, they had bunches of irises and tiger lilies, tall vases filled with pink and red gladiolas, baskets of bright orange and yellow daisies, and swags of ivy and jasmine to drape from every wall.

"I want to do an all-red arrangement," Jolie said, reaching for red roses, red tulips, and red carnations.

Miranda grinned at her. "Cool. I'll do one that's all blue. These cornflowers are too gorgeous to pass up."

Lizzie was just reaching for some pink lilies when the door to the potting shed flew open and a furious-looking Kate Sanders stalked in.

"There you are!" she said to Hal.

Hal's green eyes narrowed. "I can't believe you actually followed me here."

"I saw you get on the bus," Kate said.

"So you're the one who called him," Miranda said.

"So what?" the Evil One demanded.

Lizzie had had it with all the mystery. "Why were you following Hal?"

"None of your business, McGuire," Kate snapped.

Hal said, "Kate and I are cousins."

"That's none of their business, either," Kate said furiously.

Hal met her gaze calmly. "They deserve an explanation." He stepped out of the way of a drip. "As the whole world knows by now, Kate is getting ready for her big debutante ball next fall."

Actually, I didn't know. That might be because the she-beast and I aren't exactly best buds.

Hal saw the blank looks on Miranda's and Lizzie's faces. "Well, it's going to be a big, formal deal. And Kate's mother hired an instructor to give Kate, her groupies—"

"They are not groupies!" Kate spluttered. "They're my friends!"

"Whatever," Hal said. "The point is, Kate, her crew, plus me and my older brothers, are all supposed to be taking ballroom dancing lessons."

"*Supposed to* is right," Kate spat. "You missed last Saturday's class, and now it looks as if you're planning to miss today's."

Hal smiled thinly. "Smart girl. You're catching on."

Lizzie and Miranda exchanged a glance. They'd never seen anyone stand up to Kate so calmly. The Ice Queen had finally met her match.

Kate, though, hadn't given up. "My mother paid a lot of money for these lessons," she said. "And she guaranteed Monsieur Henri ten students.

That means we're counting on you to be there."

"Then it's too bad no one bothered to ask me if that's what I wanted. News flash: it's not." Hal looked imploringly at the others. "I mean, they expect me to *waltz*!"

"I hear you, dude," Ethan said. "Like, I feel your pain."

Kate was so furious she grabbed a gladiola stalk and broke it in two. "Hal Walters, you are a selfish, immature, stubborn—"

"Wait a minute," Lizzie said. "Does this mean that you two haven't been working together to wreck the decorations for the dance?"

Kate shot her a look of disbelief. "Oh, please! As if I would waste my time on anything so juvenile!" A huge raindrop splatted onto Kate's head and dripped down her nose.

Go rain!
Finally—you're useful!

Kate gave her cousin one last scathing look. "Fine, I'll just tell my mother you're too busy to attend my ball."

"That would be great!" Hal said happily as Kate stormed back out.

Gordo gave a low whistle. "I gotta hand it to you, man, you stood up to the she-beast."

Hal grimaced. "Trust me, I've had lots of practice." He turned to Lizzie, a look of betrayal on his face. "How could you accuse me of working with the family witch? I mean, can't you tell that I have much better taste than that?"

"Actually," Lizzie said, "I can't figure you out at all. And someone's been trashing all our work."

"It couldn't have been Hal." Miranda sounded positive. "But, Jolie, I can't help wondering about you. I mean, you could have posted that really mean message on the school Web site. And you and me, we've sort of had—a rivalry—and you liked those chili lights—"

"I would never sabotage Spring Fling!" Jolie

cried. "I can't wait for the dance. My vintage dress came, and it fits me perfectly. Plus, I've found the perfect bag, one with little beagles in silhouette that's the exact same color as the flowers on the dress, so I was going to bring it and show everyone tonight!"

"Okay, that was an extremely strange group of facts," Lizzie said, "but I don't think you're lying." Jolie might be a ditz but she was totally sincere.

"What about you, Gordo?" Jolie asked, her cheeks still red with indignation.

"Me?" Gordo asked.

"You have that toolbox," Jolie pointed out. "So you could have been the one who tore apart the arch." She sniffed. "Besides, we all had access to the gym. I think we should all be questioned."

"Sounds fair," Ethan said. "I didn't do it because flowers aren't my thing."

"Got that," Gordo said. "Look, I admit, I wasn't that keen when Miranda drafted me to work on the dance. But I never would have sabotaged it. Lizzie and Miranda are my best friends. As for the arch, I worked way too hard just to get that thing to stand up. There's no way I would destroy it."

Lizzie ducked out from beneath a drip and spoke up next. "Ever since that note was posted on the Web site, I've been trying to find the culprit. It would seriously mess up my investigation if I were the one to blame."

Did that even make sense?

She tried again. "I mean, I'd have to be a split personality or something to sabotage the dance."

"So are you?" Jolie asked.

Lizzie rolled her eyes. "I think we can also assume that Miranda wouldn't sabotage her own project. So, Hal, that brings us back to you."

Hal wasn't looking at any of them. He was weaving a swag of purple wisteria, lavender freesias, and white daisies.

"You know," he said in an odd, detached tone, "none of you ever asked me why I left my old school, Blackstone."

"Okay, why?" Miranda asked.

He put the flowers down, and his green eyes locked on Miranda's brown ones. "I was kicked out," he said. "After I trimmed all the Blackstone hedges into the shape of my favorite comic book heroes."

"Cool!" said Ethan approvingly. "You're an artist, dude!"

Which was the truth, Lizzie realized. Despite his bad-boy streak, Hal was a born artist.

Hal grinned and said, "Well, I can tell you the hedges were greatly improved when I finished with them."

"I don't get it," Miranda said. "What has this got to do with the dance?"

"It's the way I am," Hal said quietly. "When I see a chance to—rearrange things—I can't resist. Besides, I kind of was hoping to get tossed out of Hillridge, too."

"Why?" Lizzie asked.

"Kate has been trying to boss me since the day I was born. It's bad enough we're related and our families are always going to dinners and charity functions together. I didn't want to be in the same school with her, too. So I thought I'd cause some trouble, get caught, and my folks would find another school for me. That's why I hacked into the Web site and left that message," he explained. "I figured Kate would get blamed, and she'd figure out it was me. That way I'd upset my darling cousin and get my ticket out, all in one. But it didn't work that way." He bit his lip, then met Miranda's eyes. "I'm sorry, Miranda. That was a terrible thing to do to you."

Miranda was shaking with anger. "What else did you do?"

"I didn't have anything to do with the sprinklers going off," Hal said quickly.

"We know," Lizzie said. "Mr. Zaber told us it was a cracked valve."

"But I did pick the lock on Mr. Zaber's closet, which is how we kept getting his ladder and why he was upset about it," Hal explained.

"You pick locks?" Gordo asked.

"I taught myself from Internet articles." Hal shrugged. "Blackstone was boring. I needed something to do."

"Did you change the lights and empty the pails?" Lizzie demanded.

"Guilty and guilty." Hal's handsome face flushed dark red. For the first time he looked embarrassed. "It was all part of my plan to get thrown out of Hillridge. I figured someone had heard about my pranks at Blackstone."

"What about the arch?" Lizzie asked.

Hal hung his head and nodded, ashamed.

"But why did you do it?" Lizzie asked.

Hal's voice was very quiet when he answered. "I was mad."

"That's rich," Miranda said angrily. "*You* were mad at *us?*"

Hal shook his head. "At my parents. The morning we came in early to take down the lights, I realized how much I actually liked working on the dance—it was all about being creative. So I got some ferns to decorate with. Unfortunately, my dad saw me taking them from the park. He was sick of my complaints about Kate's dancing class. Plus, Mrs. Forte, the art teacher, had called and asked permission for me to add an art class. When my dad saw me with the ferns, it was the last straw. He's always envisioned me being a lawyer, like him, and doing things like going to black-tie parties. So, he called me at school, and I got a big lecture about how I had to apply myself, which meant no art class."

"But I saw you in the art room, working on a painting," Lizzie said.

"That's because Mrs. Forte lets me paint during lunch hour. My dad said I'd have to take an economics course instead. As if that wasn't bad enough, I'd have to quit the posse and join the debate club. To top it off, I had to go to a tuxedo fitting for Kate's ball. I got really upset and decided that if I couldn't work on the posse, no one would."

Hal touched Miranda's wrist. "I'm sorry, Miranda. I had a lot to work through, but I was really selfish and I'm really sorry. It was totally unfair to you and the rest of the posse."

Miranda pulled her wrist away. "No argument there."

Lizzie couldn't quite believe it. "So you opened the rabbits' cages, too?"

"Yep." Hal looked up and slid away from another leak.

"That was kind of my fault," Jolie said in a small voice. "I didn't know Mr. Pettus had bunnies in his classroom until we brought the flowers up there. And then I saw them, and they were so adorable. I really, really wanted to hold one. So I told Hal, and he said he could open the cage for me. We never meant for them to eat the flowers, honest. I just wanted to pet them."

"Then why didn't you put the rabbits back in the cage?" Lizzie asked.

"We did," Jolie insisted. "But we heard someone coming down the hall, so we just took off—"

"—before we could lock the cage again," Hal finished. "I never thought the rabbits would get out on their own, but I guess they were hungry."

He drew a ragged breath. "So I guess you all hate me now. And that's the worst, because the other thing I figured out is that I really like all of you. And except for the family witch, Hillridge is a pretty cool place to be."

"Right on!" Ethan said.

Lizzie went up to Miranda. "What do you want to do?" she whispered.

Miranda glanced at her watch. "Omigosh,"

she said, "the dance is five hours away. This is no time to hold grudges. We've got to get these flowers into the gym." She looked up at the posse. "I need all of you—even you, Hal—if we're going to bring Flower Power to Spring Fling."

"I'm there," Hal said, smiling.

The shed door opened again and Valerie peered in. "Hey, guys," she said. Her eyes lit up as she saw their work. "I've got to deliver some flowers, so if you want to pile yourselves and these gorgeous arrangements into my van, I'll drop you all at Hillridge. And," she added, "I could use an assistant, so if any of you flower artists wants to apply for the job, I'd be pretty thrilled."

Lizzie and Miranda got out of Mr. Sanchez's car, thanked him for the ride, and turned to face the school building. Miranda was wearing a lavender flower-print camisole over a three-quarter-length violet skirt, with flowers cut into the eyelet lace. Lizzie wore a short turquoise dress that had hot pink flowers twining from shoulder to hip, and a turquoise flower in her hair.

"This is it!" Miranda said, a thrill of excitement in her voice. "Flower Power, here we come!"

"Miranda." Lizzie's voice was hushed. "Do you notice something? Something almost miraculous?"

"Um, not really," Miranda admitted.

Lizzie leaped straight up into the air. "It's not raining anymore!" she cried.

Miranda patted her hair. "Omigosh. I can't believe it. I have finally exited the State of Frizz. I was beginning to think it was permanent."

Laughing, the two friends joined the stream of other kids heading toward the dance.

Spring Fling was flinging, and Lizzie and Miranda were standing in a luminous, twilit garden that just happened to be a gym. It was truly beautiful, Lizzie thought. And everyone looked as though they were having a great time. The Tudge and his girlfriend, Greta, were dancing up a storm. Neither one was terribly coordinated, but they didn't seem to care. The Ice Queen and her evil crew were over by the bleachers, being snobby together. And Jolie was talking over the music, happily showing another girl her beagle purse.

"You really pulled it off," Lizzie told Miranda. "The gym is totally transformed and everyone is having a blast."

"Yeah," Miranda said happily. "Despite the disasters, it all worked out. Speaking of disasters . . ." She nodded toward the entry where Hal was just coming into the gym.

They watched as he headed toward Jolie, casually putting an arm around her shoulders.

"That doesn't bother you?" Lizzie asked. "I mean, Hal and Jolie."

"Hal may be hot, but he's not for me," Miranda explained. "I always felt like we were competing for who had the best idea. Besides, with all that weird stuff he pulled, I can't figure out what he really is—an amazing artist or a criminal mastermind."

Lizzie watched Hal say something to Jolie,

then walk toward them. "He's kind of messed up," Lizzie agreed, "but I think that deep down he's basically decent. It sounds like he's trying to figure out a lot of stuff."

"Hey," Hal said. "I just wanted to tell you how incredible the place looks, and to apologize again. And also to tell you that I talked to my dad. He agreed that I could apply for that job with Ethan's aunt. He said maybe it wouldn't be so bad for me to have a constructive outlet for my—uh—skills."

"I think it sounds like a great idea," Lizzie said.

"Especially if it gets me out of ballroom-dancing classes," Hal agreed. "In any case, I'm giving up the destructo act."

"That sounds promising," Miranda said with a smile.

"There you are!" Jolie appeared at Hal's side and looped her arm through his. She was wearing a cute vintage dress—white cotton with a full skirt and a print of big, red flowers. She even wore red flower earrings and a matching necklace.

"Perfect threads!" Miranda told her.

Jolie grinned. "Perfect party, Miranda. I'm getting people to take photos with their cell phones, then I'm going to post them on a Flower Power page for the school Web site." She turned to Lizzie. "Do you want to see my new purse?"

"Um, maybe later," Lizzie said. She had just spotted Ethan. He was standing by the refreshments table, talking into Gordo's camcorder.

Ethan's telling Gordo his dating secrets! I definitely want instant replay.

Miranda nudged Lizzie. "Go on," she said. "Ask him to dance."

Fear filled Lizzie's heart. "I'm not sure I can," she said in a small voice. "I'm still scarred by rejection."

"Well, don't be," Miranda said. "The rain has stopped, and it's all good. This is your big chance."

Slowly, Lizzie worked her way toward Ethan and Gordo. She figured that if Ethan ignored her, she could always pretend it was Gordo she had come to talk to. But when she was about a foot away from them, Gordo said, "Later, man," and walked off to interview the leader of the marching band.

Ethan's eyes met Lizzie's. He looked extra hot tonight, Lizzie thought, in khakis and a flowered Hawaiian shirt.

Remember: just be cool, casual, and sophisticated.

"Dude," Ethan said.

"Hi," Lizzie said back.

And don't forget, wow him with witty dialogue.

"Want to dance?" Ethan asked.

Lizzie felt her eyes widen in astonishment. "Me?"

Ethan didn't answer. He took her hand and drew her toward him. Lizzie felt him rest one hand lightly on her back, the other on her waist. She suddenly became aware of the music. It was a sweet, slow ballad.

Omigosh, I'm slow-dancing with Ethan Craft! So this is what heaven feels like.

She almost stepped on his foot and caught herself. Lizzie was almost swooning with the romance of it all. This was even better than running toward each other in slow motion.

Suddenly, Lizzie felt a cold metal rim against her calf.

Oh, no! In the next breath Lizzie stumbled backward and she and Ethan fell onto one of the buckets filled with water and floating orchids.

Lizzie, who had been so happy about the rains stopping, was soaked once again. Her dress, shoes, legs—everything was drenched! Lizzie shut her eyes. Her Spring Fling had become Spring Sploosh!

"Hey, dude."

Lizzie cautiously opened one eye to see Ethan removing a drippy orchid from his lap. He got to his feet and held out a hand to her.

Lizzie couldn't take any more. How did her most romantic moment ever turn into total humiliation? She shook her head. "I can't," she said.

"Sure you can." Ethan grinned at her, took her hand, and pulled her to her feet. "It's a rockin' great party, Lizzie," he told her. "Let's dance!"